Storytime
for
4
year olds

by JOAN STIMSON

illustrated by
JOHN and CAROLINE ASTROP

Ladybird

Ernest takes a ride

Ernest the elephant had an ambition.
He wanted to ride on a red bus.

Each day Ernest looked out from his
enclosure. The buses went by exactly on the
hour. 'The three o'clock is the bus for me,'
thought Ernest. 'Everyone will be taking a
nap after lunch.'

Then he made his Plan.

One morning Mr Wainwright found a new
notice in Ernest's enclosure.

Throw cash, not buns. Am saving up.
signed *Ernest Elephant*

Mr Wainwright was shocked – but the visitors loved it. In just one day Ernest became rich.

That night Ernest went to bed early, but he was too excited to sleep.

'Tomorrow,' he kept thinking, 'I shall ride on a red bus.'

Ernest was too nervous to eat breakfast. He was too jittery to take lunch. He was beginning to think that three o'clock would never come.

By five minutes to three Mr Wainwright and the animals were snoring.

Heave! By two minutes to three Ernest had clambered onto the boundary wall of the zoo.

It was a real struggle, but Ernest made it.

At exactly three o'clock the red bus arrived at the zoo. Ernest dangled his trunk over the wall, right by the bus stop.

Contents

Ladybird books are widely available, but in case of
difficulty may be ordered by post or telephone from:

Ladybird Books – Cash Sales Department
Littlegate Road Paignton Devon TQ3 3BE
Telephone 0803 554761

A catalogue record for this book is available
from the British Library

Published by Ladybird Books Ltd Loughborough Leicestershire UK
Ladybird Books Inc Auburn Maine 04210 USA

Eeek! The bus driver screeched to a halt. Ernest had attracted his attention all right. His trunk was blocking the road!

The bus had an open top, which lined up perfectly with the zoo wall, and Ernest stepped very gently on board. Then he settled comfortably into six or seven seats.

The bus driver had got over his surprise, and he was beginning to feel quite important. He was looking forward to telling the other drivers he'd picked up an elephant!

7

The bus conductor was beginning to feel nervous. What if the elephant didn't have the fare? But he needn't have worried. Ernest had *plenty* of money. He handed it over with a note:

Return trip to the zoo – keep the change.
        signed *Ernest Elephant*

The red bus drove through the country and into town. Ernest saw all the sights – the shops, the churches, the parks and the factories. He'd done it at last!

'I'm riding on a red bus, I'm riding on a red bus,' hummed Ernest happily.

Every few minutes the bus stopped. An old lady got on with her dog. A young boy got off with his hamster.

But there were no zebras, monkeys, seals or hippos at the bus stops. There was no sign of Mr Wainwright's friendly face. Ernest began to feel homesick – homesick and *hungry*.

At exactly four o'clock the red bus pulled up outside the zoo.

Ernest got up from his six or seven seats, and stepped gently back onto the zoo wall.

Thud! Ernest was back in his enclosure.

Mr Wainwright and the animals had stopped snoring. They were beginning to stir.

'It's great to be home,' thought Ernest, and nuzzled his trunk into Mr Wainwright's ear. Then he gave Mr Wainwright a playful push.

Mr Wainwright didn't need a note to know what Ernest wanted. Mr Wainwright could read Ernest like a book.

Ernest wanted his tea!

The
Jumble
Sale

The Jumble Sale

Russell woke up and wriggled. Then he saw the knot in his middle. And remembered.

'Snakes alive!' cried Russell. 'It's the day of the Jumble Sale.'

All morning Russell rummaged in his room. Soon his rucksack was full. Before long his shelves were empty.

Then Russell shook his moneybox. 'I won't want to *buy* anything,' said Russell. 'Not now my room's so tidy.' But he took some money along – just in case.

The Church Hall was packed. 'Thank you, Russell,' beamed the vicar's wife. She arranged Russell's things on a stall. Russell slithered up a table leg – to get a better view.

Russell didn't enjoy seeing his things being sold.

'*Special offer!*' cried one of the helpers suddenly.

Russell rushed over to look. 'Ooh, I haven't read these,' he cried. He reached for some adventure stories.

'What about *Snakes & Ladders*?' asked another helper.

'Yes, *please!*' said Russell. Soon his rucksack was full. Before long he'd spent all his money.

Russell slid slowly home. He arranged his new collection of books and games. He took a leisurely bath.

Russell yawned and wriggled into bed, then he looked across at his shelves. 'There's no point in having shelves with nothing on them,' he said.

And, of course, Russell was right.

Happy

Happy is buying a brand new balloon.
Happy is jelly heaped high on a spoon.

Happy is riding an old steam train.
Happy is giggling again and again.

Happy is climbing a favourite tree –
Look! A ladybird's landed on me.

Happy is playing with my best friend.
Happy is choosing which present to send.

Happy is feeling the wind in my hair –
I'm riding my bike as fast as I dare.

Happy is Dad playing cricket with me.
Happy is cuddling as close as can be.

Happy is four, looking forward to five –
Happy is fun! I'm GLAD I'm alive.

Noisy Norman

'Little tortoises should be seen and not heard.' But you couldn't help hearing Norman! Norman was so *noisy*.

Whenever Norman wanted to say anything, he yelled and shrieked. Whenever Norman went anywhere, he crashed and banged.

'I do wish Norman didn't get up so *early*,' said Mrs T. 'It's such a long day with all that noise.'

Mr T. had a bright idea. 'Let's get Norman a paper round. Paper boys start at the crack of dawn.'

Norman liked his new job. But he didn't just deliver the papers. He rattled the letterboxes and yelled, 'READ ALL ABAHT IT, READ ALL ABAHT IT!' – at the top of his voice.

Nobody wanted to read all about it – not at six o'clock in the morning. Norman got the sack.

'I do wish Norman didn't go to bed so *late*,' said Mrs T. 'It's such a long day with all that noise.'

Mr T. had another idea. 'Norman can join a band. Musicians are meant to be noisy. And they work late.'

The band leader gave Norman a triangle. He explained what to do – 'Wait for the pianist to finish playing. Then go *"ting, ting, ting."*'

But Norman couldn't wait for the pianist to finish. As soon as the music started, he went *'crash, bang, wallop!'* He jumped up and down and shrieked out of tune.

The pianist was annoyed. The band leader was unhappy. He asked Norman to leave the band.

Mr T. had run out of ideas, so Mrs T. took Norman to the doctor.

The doctor jumped when Norman crashed into his surgery. He covered his ears when Norman yelled 'HELLO!'

'I need some *whisper* medicine for Norman,' said Mrs T.

The doctor looked through his catalogue.

'I'm sorry,' he said. '*Whisper* medicine hasn't been invented yet.' The doctor wrote something on a piece of paper and gave it to Mrs T.

It turned out to be the name of a karate school, and Mrs T. fixed up karate lessons straightaway.

'Now you can jump up and down *and* be noisy,' she told Norman.

'Just watch the others,' said the instructor. 'You can join in next week.'

But Norman couldn't wait for next week. 'LOOK AT MEEEEEE!' he shrieked at the top of his voice – and his cry shattered the windows in the karate hall.

The instructor was shattered too, and he sent Norman home with a note. It said, *'Don't ever send Norman again!'*

Neither Mr T. nor Mrs T. knew what to do next. Then the fair came to town.

'Off you go, Norman,' said Mrs T. 'You can be as noisy as you like at the fair.'

Norman jumped up and down with excitement. He was *even noisier* than usual.

'I WANT TO GO ON THE DODGEMS,' yelled Norman. And suddenly ALL the dodgems were full.

'I'VE WON A COCONUT,' shrieked Norman. And suddenly *everyone* was at the coconut shy.

'LOVELY LANDY LOSS,' cried Norman. Even with his mouth full, Norman could be heard all over the fairground. There was soon a *huge queue* for the candy floss.

The fairground manager came to see Norman's parents. 'We don't need to advertise with Norman about,' said the manager. 'Can you spare him for a few evenings?'

What a wonderful arrangement! Norman's big voice brought big business to the fair. And Mr and Mrs T. had a rest – from *Norman's noise*!

Just the
job for
a dragon

Just the job for a dragon

Dilys read the advertisement in the café window.

WANTED –
Smart young lady to wait at table

'Just the job for a dragon,' thought Dilys, and stepped inside.

The café manager wasn't so sure. 'We'll have to see how you get on,' he said.

Dilys helped the cook to peel the potatoes. Then she flew round setting the tables.

At twelve o'clock the first customers arrived. Dilys stood by their table with notepad and pencil.

'I can feel a draught,' cried Grandma Grumble. 'Right on my feet.'

'I *am* sorry, Madame,' said Dilys. She lifted the cloth and dived under the table. Then she took a deep breath. 'PUFF!' Dilys blew hot air all over Grandma Grumble's toes.

'Ooh, that's lovely,' gurgled Grandma Grumble.

The Grumbles read the menu. 'It all sounds horrible,' they said. But they ordered a huge meal, just the same.

Dilys brought out their plates. Mr and Mrs Grumble poked and prodded. 'These plates are cold!' they cried. 'Hot food should be served on hot plates.'

'I *do* apologise, Sir *and* Madame,' said Dilys.

Dilys collected up the plates and turned her back. 'PUFF!' She aimed a great flame right at the plates, and took them back to the table.

'Ouch!' cried Mr and Mrs Grumble. 'These plates are *piping hot*!'

The Grumbles ate their main course. But Sidney wanted his pudding.

'Bring me a Spaceship Special,' he cried.

'Banana, jelly, nuts, ice cream...' the cook made up the Spaceship Special – but he forgot to light the sparkler on top.

'My sparkler's gone out!' wailed Sidney.

'Oh no, it hasn't!' said Dilys.

'PUFF!' She sent a gentle flame right onto the spaceship, and the sparkler crackled into life.

'Crikey!' said Sidney.

The Grumbles paid their bill with hardly a grumble. Dilys began to clear the table.

'What do you think?' she asked the manager.

'I think,' said the manager, 'that this is *just the job for a dragon*!'

The
greedy
camel

The greedy camel

Graham's favourite food was spaghetti. His favourite word was 'MORE.'

'Don't be so greedy, Graham,' said Mrs Camel. 'You'll get a spare tyre.'

Most mothers couldn't face feeding Graham. But when his best friend Stanley had a birthday, he said, 'I don't want a party unless Graham can come.'

So Stanley's Mum had to prepare a huge birthday tea. 'I do hope Graham won't eat *everyone's* share,' she thought. Then she had a brainwave. She let the other boys start first.

At last Graham was allowed to join in.
He forked up the spaghetti. He ate up all
the fish fingers. He polished off the pies and
gobbled the gateau.

Everyone had a small slice of birthday
cake. And Graham
ate the rest.

'I feel full!' said Graham when he went to bed that night. He still felt full next morning.

Graham heard the doorbell ring.

'Stanley's here,' called Mrs Camel. 'He's come to play football.'

Graham put on his football jersey. It did feel funny. Then he went downstairs.

Stanley stood and stared at Graham.
Mrs Camel couldn't believe her eyes.

Graham didn't have a spare tyre. He had
grown a *spare hump*. No wonder his football
jersey felt funny! But he still went out to play.

'The exercise will do you good,' said
Mrs Camel. 'And there will be *no more
spaghetti* – until that extra hump has gone!'

Ten crazy crabs

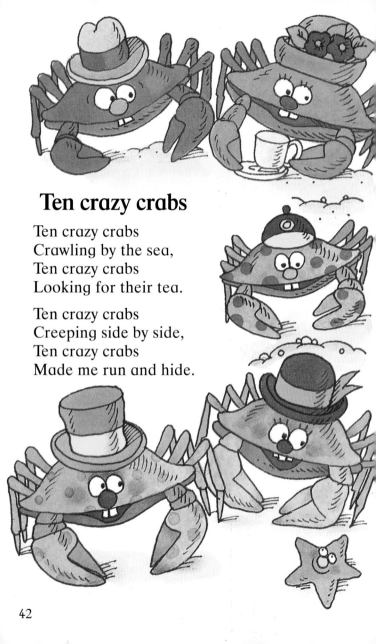

Ten crazy crabs

Ten crazy crabs
Crawling by the sea,
Ten crazy crabs
Looking for their tea.

Ten crazy crabs
Creeping side by side,
Ten crazy crabs
Made me run and hide.

Ten crazy crabs
Hungry for some toes,
Help! Crazy crabs –
I've got TEN of those.

Ten crazy crabs
Made me want to scream.
Then I woke up –
What a crazy dream!

43